Easter Eggs for Anya

A Ukrainian Celebration of New Life in Christ

Written by Virginia Kroll

Illustrated by Sally Wern Comport

zonderkidz

With love to my cherished granddaughter, Hannah Pellette
—V.K.

To Theresa, my sister-in-law and sister in life,
whom I adore; unfailing in devotion to family
—S.W.C.

zonderkidz
The children's group
of Zondervan

www.zonderkidz.com

Easter Eggs for Anya
Copyright © 2007 by Virginia Kroll
Illustrations © 2007 by Sally Wern Comport

Requests for information should be addressed to:
Grand Rapids, Michigan 49530

ISBN 10: 0-310-71079-0
ISBN 13: 978-0-31071079-0

Editor: Amy De Vries
Art direction: Laura Maitner Mason

The body text for this book is set in Goudy Old Style.

Printed in China

07 08 09 10 11 • 10 9 8 7 6 5 4 3 2 1

The angel said to the women, "Do not be afraid,
for I know that you are looking for Jesus, who was crucified.
He is not here; he has risen, just as he said."

—Matthew 28:5-6a

Author's Note

The art of *pysanky* (pi-SAH-nkey) eggs originated in the Ukraine. For centuries, girls and women all over Eastern Europe and Russia have decorated Easter eggs in a variety of intricate, sometimes mosaic, designs. Today, the artist pokes holes in each end of a raw egg, and blows out the contents. Then she draws designs on the egg with a special tool called a stylus or a *kistka* (kiss-kuh) that is dipped in melted beeswax. But back when this story takes place, in the early 1900s, the insides were not blown out. The yolk and the shell symbolize life, so it was important to the Ukrainians to leave the egg intact.

Eggs are decorated with popular secular symbols such as the sun (for good luck), chickens (for wishes), flowers (for affection and beauty), birds (for the coming of springtime), and horses or deer (for health and wealth). Eggs are also decorated with Christian symbols. A cross signifies the Resurrection of Christ. Dots depict Mary's tears. A fish denotes sacrifice and, therefore, stands for Jesus and his followers. Circles are signs of eternity because they have no beginning and no end. Hearts stand for love, and stars symbolize God's love for people. A triangle is the symbol for the Trinity (Father, Son, and Holy Spirit), and if crisscrossed with netting, it symbolizes Christ and the fishermen.

In Ukraine, Christians go to church late on Easter Saturday night. It is the custom to exchange brightly decorated pysanky eggs with friends and family. The eggs are given with the greeting, "Christ is risen!"

Anya crept to her "praying place" under the hay wagon and pulled her skirts around her for warmth. Even though it was time for spring to spread its sunshine over the Ukraine, the wind was still wintry and the sky was slate-gray.

"Dear Jesus," Anya prayed, "help our garden grow again, and let Mashenka give lots of milk." As she thought of sugar beets and boiled, buttered cabbage, her mouth watered. "Easter will be different this year with Papa away at war. We don't even have any eggs to turn into colored treasures. Please forgive me for feeling sad. And help me to remember that you bring new life."

A frightful honking shattered Anya's quiet moment. A great gray-lag goose rose up, hissing and flapping its frantic wings at a lunging fox.

"Fly!" Anya shouted, but the goose held her ground. Anya raced toward the fox, flailing her arms and yelling, but the snarling fox was too quick. The fox lunged once more and dragged off its feathered meal.

Anya's eyes stung with tears. *The goose's mate must be dead too*, she thought, *or he'd have helped her guard their nest. Now their eggs will never hatch*, she sighed. The eggs were getting cold. Four of them lay orphaned in a circle of straw. But even in her sadness, Anya understood that the fox and her babies were hungry too. Then she recognized the sudden gift she had been given.

Anya pulled the folded kerchief, her babushka, from her head and spread it on the ground. She gently placed the eggs in it, cushioning them with the dried grass and soft down feathers from the goose's nest. Then she carefully wrapped them up. Anya held the eggs close to her. Even though the wind whipped her hair over her red-cheeked face, she felt warmed by her swirling thoughts. She would have Easter eggs after all!

Since Anya had been a baby, she had watched Mama make pysanky eggs. Last year she had decorated her own egg for the first time. Mama had said that Anya worked fast, and Papa had agreed that she had a true artist's touch.

Anya would decorate an egg for everyone in her family. When she presented the eggs, she'd use the greeting "Christ is risen!" as Mama and Papa had taught her.

Hoping she would not be noticed, Anya slipped through the door. "Anya," called Mama without turning around, "please tend to Jarek while I finish the bread."

"Yes, Mama," she replied.

Anya hurried to her room. She took her rag doll, Dasha, from her basket and tucked her precious new bundle into it instead. Then she ran to Jarek's room, and made him laugh by using Dasha as a puppet.

After supper and chores, Anya lay in bed, snugging Dasha and thanking God for the unexpected blessing. Tomorrow she would clean the eggs to get them ready. She pictured her egg-decorating supplies, tucked safely away on the top pantry shelf. Her heart pounded extra hard as she imagined the different designs she would put on each egg—fishes and flowers, hearts and hens, suns and stars, and most important, crosses.

"An egg for Mama, one for Jarek, and I'll save Papa's till he gets home," she whispered to her doll. She smiled. "That leaves the last one for you, Dasha."

Anya fell asleep thinking, *Our home without Papa is like the goose's nest without her gander.*

As dawn crept through her window, Anya heard the faintest crackle, like a beetle clicking. She listened hard again, but heard nothing. She shrugged and pulled on her sweater. Then she heard another sound, like the "tick" of a pebble against a wagon wheel. Anya knelt beside the basket and unwrapped her babushka.

"NO!" she wailed.

Every one of her eggs was cracked. But how? She'd been *so* careful.

Mama rushed in. "What happened?" she cried.

Anya spilled out her tale and her tears against Mama's nightgown. "Now we won't have any Easter eggs!" she sputtered between sobs.

"You're right," Mama said. "We'll have something better."

Anya heard a smile in Mama's voice. As Anya raised her puzzled face, Mama turned it toward the basket.

A small beak with a hard white tip pecked at the shell, which cracked like the ice on Petrovskys' pond during the springtime thaw.

Three more gray-lag goslings emerged. They were wet and tired from hatching, but strong and ready to meet the world at Eastertime.

"Now we'll have feathers for pillows and quilts." Mama said.

"And Easter eggs forever!" Anya cried.

Suddenly she and Mama heard a knocking sound.

"Oh dear!" exclaimed Mama. "We've wakened Jarek."

"I'll get him, Mama," Anya offered.

But Jarek was still fast asleep. The banging came again.

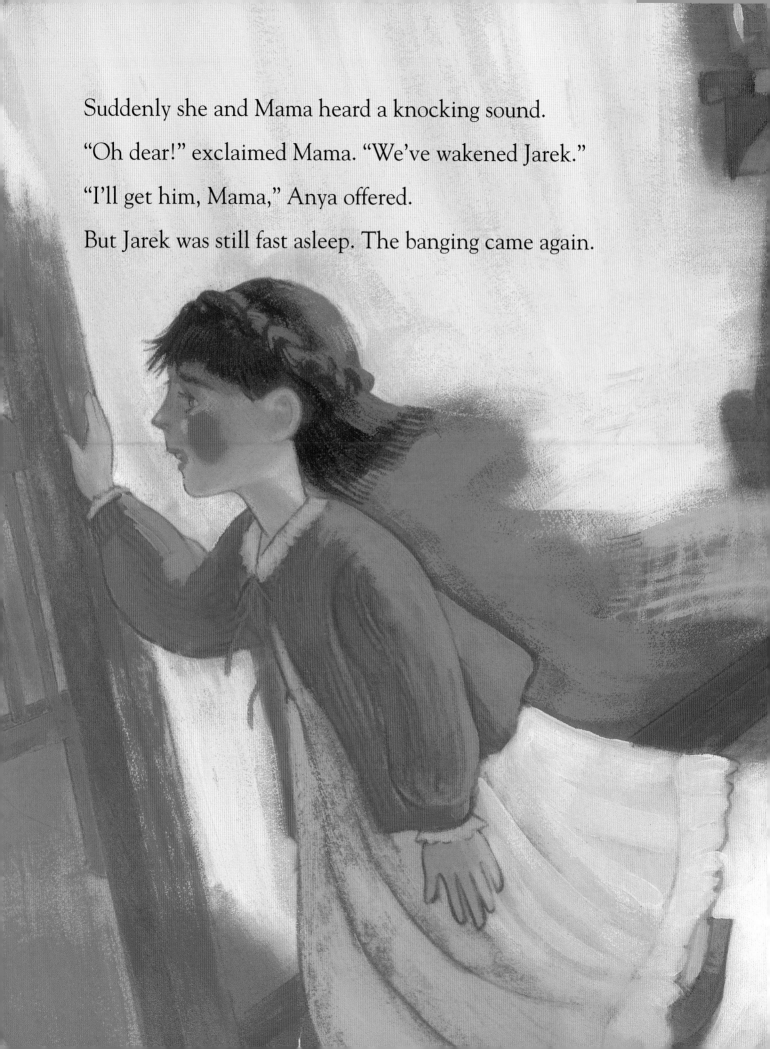

"Mama, it's the door," said Anya.

Mama frowned. "Who would knock this early?" She clasped her shawl at her neck with one hand and slowly unlatched the door with the other.

Anya heard Mama gasp. Then her arms raised, and the shawl spilled down Mama's back like a waterfall.

Anya noticed a man's arm leaning on a crutch and his other circling Mama's waist. Then peering over Mama's shoulder, she saw the familiar face. "Papa!" Anya cried, running to join the hug.

"Happy Easter!" Papa's voice thundered through their home.

Anya ran to the basket, and cupped a gosling in her hands.

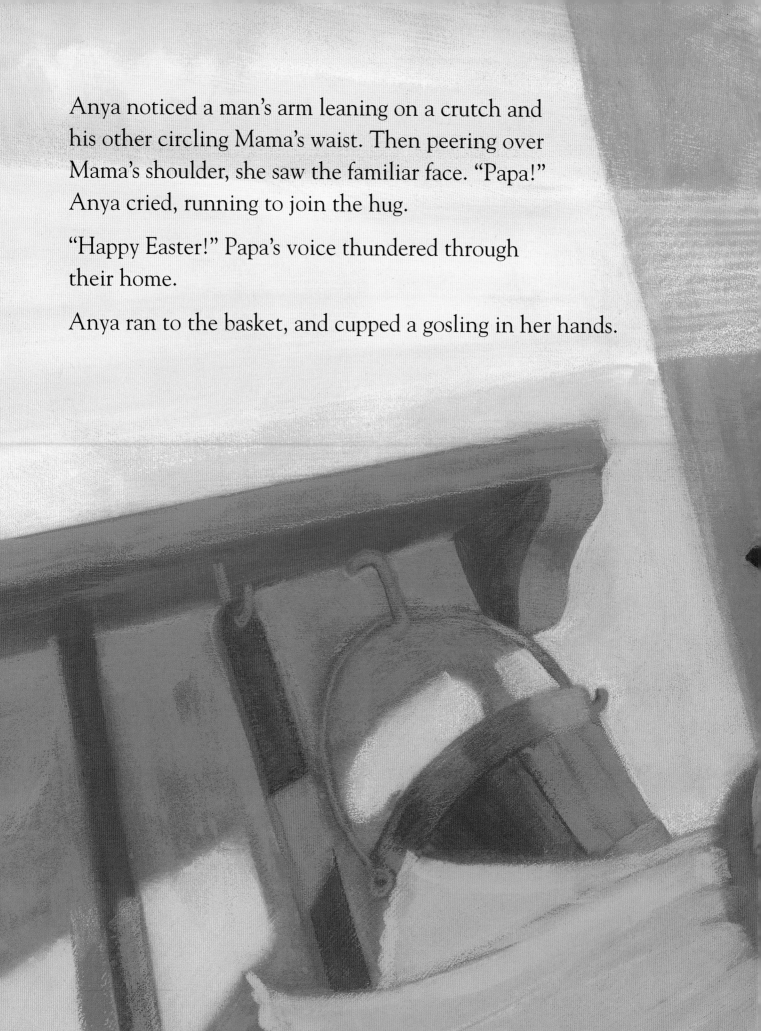

"Christ is risen!" Anya said, giving the gosling to Papa.

"Indeed!" Papa heartily agreed.

He had a surprise for Anya too. He reached into his bag and pulled out a small box. "Be very careful," he said quietly.

Anya unwrapped the oval treasure. "Oh, Papa!" she squealed. "An egg all ready for me to decorate! Thank you!"

Later, Anya would tell Papa the whole story about the goose, the fox, and the goslings. Later, too, she would decorate the most special pysanky egg of all, the only pysanky egg of the year.

But first she had to do something more important.

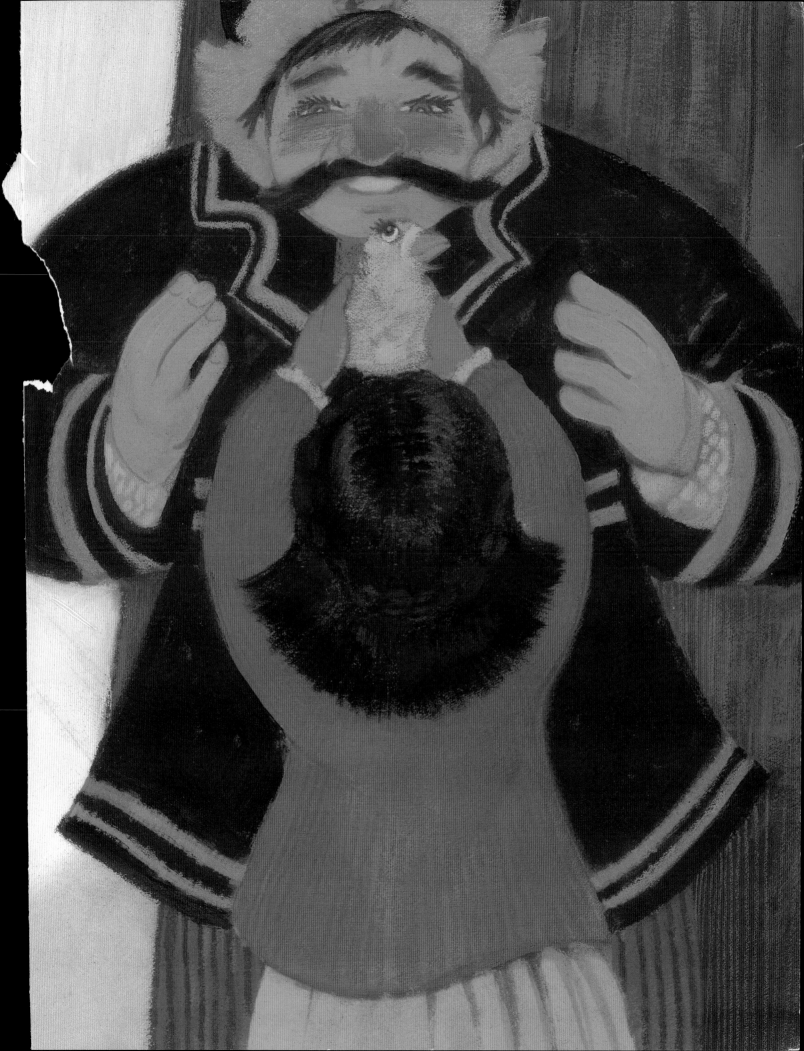

Anya went outside, squinting at the brilliant sunshine. Suddenly she noticed that the yard was dotted with creamy snowdrops, and one golden crocus had blossomed near the door. Anya crept to her "praying place" and crossed her arms over her heart. "Thank you, Jesus!" she said, "for this season of new life!"

As echoes of gentle honking filled the clear morning sky, Anya tingled with happiness from head to toe.

Keeping the Tradition

A Pysanky Egg of Your Own

You don't have to be an artist to create a pysanky egg. Start with a hardboiled egg. Sharpen a light-colored crayon. Draw crosses, stars, hearts, fishes, etc., in circular patterns around your egg. When you dip your egg into the darker-colored dye, the wax of the crayon will resist the dye, and your designs will show. Decorate several eggs and give them away. Remember to say "Christ is risen!" when you present them.

Easter Egg Card

Fold a piece of paper in half. Draw an oval shape like an egg and cut it out, leaving the center section of the fold uncut so your egg can be "opened." Decorate the outside of your card with crayons or markers in "pysanky," springtime symbols, and/or Easter symbols. Write an Easter message inside the card and sign your name.

Glorious Game

Draw different pysanky designs, such as a heart, a star, a fish, a bird, a triangle, a cross, etc. The symbols can be simple. Make each about two inches long. Put your designs in a basket or bowl. Take turns with friends and family members, closing your eyes and picking out a symbol. See if you can give a Bible quote or a fact that pertains to each symbol, or make up your own prayer or saying to go with the symbol you've chosen. Examples:

Heart: "God is love. Whoever lives in love lives in God, and God in him." (1 John 4:16) Or, "And now these three remain: faith, hope and love. But the greatest of these is love." (1 Corinthians 13:13)

Triangle: Jesus said, "I will make you fishers of men." (Mark 1:7)

Bird: "Look at the birds of the sky. They do not sow or reap or gather into barns, yet your heavenly Father feeds them." (Matthew 6:26) Or tell a fact about a certain songbird, such as *Robins are in the thrush family* or *Starlings can mimic other birds' calls*.

Star: "Thank you, God, for twinkling stars and a glowing moon to light our world at night."